# The Fish in
# the Bathtub

# The Fish in the Bathtub

## Eoin Colfer

With illustrations by
**Peter Bailey**

Barrington Stoke

Published in 2014 in Great Britain by
Barrington Stoke Ltd
18 Walker Street, Edinburgh, EH3 7LP

www.barringtonstoke.co.uk

This story was first published in a different form in
*Midnight Feast* (Harper Collins, 2007)

Text © 2007 Eoin Colfer
Illustrations © 2014 Peter Bailey

The moral right of Eoin Colfer and Peter Bailey to be identified
as the author and illustrator of this work has been asserted in
accordance with the Copyright, Designs and Patents Act, 1988

A CIP catalogue record for this book is available
from the British Library upon request

ISBN: 978-1-78112-360-7

Printed in China by Leo

This book has dyslexia friendly features

*To Barbara, who told me about the fish*

# Contents

# CHAPTER 1
## Grandpa's Stories

Warsaw is an old city, but its bricks and mortar are new. The German army flattened it on their way home from Poland in 1945 at the end of the war. Grandpa told Lucja this many times each week.

Every time Grandpa told the story, Lucja saw a picture in her head of a giant black boot stepping out of the sky and crushing the spires and bridges of the city.

Sometimes this picture made Lucja giggle. It was funny, like a cartoon.

Grandpa Feliks did not like it when Lucja laughed at his story.  Lucja didn't know why he got upset.  It wasn't as if his stories were true.

"Warsaw is not a city of buildings," Grandpa would insist.  "It is a city of people.  We have been here longer."

# CHAPTER 2
## Lucja

Lucja lived in a flat on Targowa Street with Grandpa Feliks and Mama Agata.

There were many other families in the building, and in these families there were at least 12 other 8-year-old girls.

Well, there may have been many more, but Lucja could only count to 12. She had never tried to count past 12. In fact, 12 was her record. By the time she got that far, she was already bored.

Lucja got bored easily, and this was why she was no good at standing in line. For the first ten seconds she was fine, but then questions would burst out of her like air from a popped balloon.

"Why is that woman so fat?" she would ask.

Or, "That man's nose is red, Mama. Why is his nose so red?"

The most embarrassing question of all was about Missus Jazinka. They were

in the line for sausages at the time. "Is there a shortage of tissues, Mama?" Lucja asked. "Because that woman just wiped her nose on her sleeve, then her sleeve on that boy's head."

Lucja's mother abandoned the line, and they ate vegetables for a few days.

"You are like an American, Lucja!" Grandpa Feliks shouted. "Everything has to be 'now' with you. This is not New York City! Here we stand in line. You must learn this in Warsaw."

"Your button is loose," said Lucja, pointing out what she saw. As she always did.

"And anyway," Lucja told Grandpa Feliks. "There was no carp last Christmas, even when you stood in line. I remember that."

It was true. Last year, Grandpa Feliks had taken on the duty of waiting in line for the fish for Christmas Eve dinner. He put newspapers in his shoes, and stood in line for six hours outside

the fish shop. But he came home without
even the smell of fish on his hands.

"That only happened once, you impertinent child," Grandpa Feliks told Lucja. "And it will not happen again. Neither Germans nor Communists will keep me from a fish steak this Christmas Eve."

"What does a German look like?"
Lucja asked.

"Like a Communist," Grandpa Feliks
said crossly.  "But with better boots."

# CHAPTER 3
# Old Ways

There were ways to get hold of things without standing in the dreaded lines.

Old ways.

Barter.

People had things and they would trade them.  These people were breaking the law.  But the Party who made the law were a long way away in Moscow, and people had to live.

Even the Party soldiers ignored the old women who wandered the streets of Warsaw with large baskets that seemed at first glance to be filled with rags.

One of these old ladies – a "veal lady" – arrived at Lucja's back door on Saint Nicholas' Day, two weeks before Christmas.  She plonked her basket on the table and drew back the cloth.  The basket was lined with plastic bags and brimming with cuts of beef and boar.

Grandpa Feliks was listening to Abba on his tape player, acting casual.

"Gin-do-bray, Adamski," the old lady said. "What can I do for you today? A nice bit of beef?"

"Fish is what I want," Grandpa Feliks said. "Carp, in fact."

The veal lady pulled up a chair. This was serious business.

"Mamma mia," she sighed, as she helped herself to a glass of water. "Here I go again. Carp, Adamski? That will cost you."

# CHAPTER 4
# A Delivery

The fish came that evening.  In a bucket.

Grandpa Feliks was surprised. "What's the bucket for?" he asked.  "I ordered carp, not a bucket."

"The bucket costs extra," the veal lady said. "The water is free. A gift for Saint Nicholas' Day."

Grandpa Feliks scowled. "I expected carp steaks wrapped in paper, packed in ice," he said.

"Ice? I don't carry ice," the veal lady said. "I'm a veal lady, not a fish lady. I don't gut or fillet. This way, you can be sure it is fresh. You want it or not?"

Grandpa Feliks passed her a small pile of coins.

"I want it," he said. "This Christmas
Eve, we eat carp before church. No
German or Communist is going to tell
me I can't eat the fish from Polish rivers.
First they took my house, then they blew
it up, then they built us this ugly block
of concrete. But I will have my carp.
You have to make a stand."

The veal lady rubbed Lucja's head,
to show she was sorry Lucja had a crazy
grandfather.

"Whatever you say, Feliks," she said.
"You and the fish can make a stand
together.  Now I need my bucket if you
don't mind."

# CHAPTER 5
# A New Home

Lucja hadn't heard a single word her grandfather or the veal lady said.

There was a fish, in a bucket, in her house.  A fish swimming in lazy figures of 8, bumping into the shiny metal.

Lucja followed her grandpa into the bathroom, where he dragged some bed-sheets from the bath and poured in the fish. It rolled from the bucket like a silver-brown tyre, then flapped for a bit until Lucja added some water.

Lucja prodded his back. "Now, Mister Carp," she said, "breathe all you like. Fish breathe water, Grandpa."

"Not for long," Grandpa Feliks muttered. He wanted to break the bad news about Mister Carp and Christmas Eve dinner in a kind way.

But Lucja wasn't interested in the hard facts of life. "He sucks the oxygen out of the water with his gills," she said. "So we have to change the water every few days."

Grandpa Feliks's eyes widened. "He? The fish is a *he* now. And where did you learn so much about fish all of a sudden?"

Lucja looked up from the bathtub. "I am 8, Grandpa. I do know stuff. I just don't know anything about history, because you're the only one who cares about that."

Grandpa Feliks searched in his pocket for some tobacco. "Sometimes I think you're right," he said, and he headed outside for a smoke.

# CHAPTER 6
# Friends

Lucja and the carp became very close.

This was odd. Not because the creature in the bath was a fat brown fish, but because before this Lucja had never sat still for more than five seconds. Her mind wandered at the speed of light.

Ideas bounced around in there like beads in a rattle.  No matter how hard she tried, Lucja could never hold on to one idea for more than a moment. Often the beginnings and endings of her sentences would have no bearing on each other.  For example –

"Mama, I am putting on my gloves because the whale song sounds so sad."

"Yes, Lucja," Mama would say. Sometimes she was sad that she could not live in her child's beautiful world herself.

So girl and fish became friends. Though it might be that the fish didn't know a thing about it. He swam about his hard white pool, and he never seemed surprised to find titbits and left-overs that had not been there the last time he passed.

Lucja sat on a kettle box beside the tub and talked to her new friend. She nodded with great interest at the replies she imagined.

"It is cold today, Fishy," she would say, and she would reach a finger into the water to stroke the single fin on the carp's back. "I suppose you are cold all the time. Maybe you like the cold. Was it cold in your egg?"

And the fish would answer, but only in Lucja's world. "No, my dear," he would say. "It was warm and soft in my egg and I wish I was there still. But as

I cannot be there, I am glad to be here, where you tickle my back and tell me important news of the outside world."

Lucja thought for a moment. "Important news. Hmm," she said. "Well, I saw a twig on the path today. It looked like a sparrow's leg. And the icicle on the fence has gone. Grandpa says one of the local louts may have snapped it off to use for mischief."

"Heavens!" the carp gasped. "Such news. The world is in such a state."

"And I have a blister," Lucja went on. "And this morning I woke up sneezing."

"Stop," the fish cried. "No more. I will be sad. Sing to me instead."

So Lucja sang a beautiful song about a cat who was using up his nine lives one

by one.  And the fish grew calm and his
swimming grew lazy and slow.

# CHAPTER 7
## Christmas Eve

This went on for two weeks.

"I cannot believe it," Mama Agata whispered. "I thought Lucja would lose interest. But she loves that carp. She sings to it. She's in there now cleaning the bathroom, for the fish."

Grandpa Feliks shook his head.
"It has to go, Agata," he said. "It is
Christmas Eve, and I will have fish for
my dinner. No Communist or German
can stop me, daughter. I am making a
stand."

Mama Agata sighed. "I know. You are right, of course. You better go in and tell her."

"M-me?" Grandpa Feliks stuttered. "I thought that you would tell her. Maybe whisk her to her room for a Christmas story."

Agata folded her arms. "You are the one who wants to make a stand, Papa," she said. "You can be the one to break Lucja's little heart."

'Break her little heart?' Grandpa Feliks thought with a scowl. It was a fish in that bathtub, not a diamond necklace.

# CHAPTER 8
## A Stand

Lucja was showing the carp a drawing of the family when Grandpa Feliks entered the bathroom.

"This is me and Mama and Grandpa," Lucja told the carp. "And there's you in the bath. I've given you a top hat because we're all going to the opera."

Then Lucja spotted Grandpa Feliks. "Oh, Grandpa, do you need to go?" she asked.

"Eh, no," said Grandpa Feliks. He was not comfortable with Lucja's habit of sharing information about bathroom habits.

"I'll leave if you do," Lucja went on. "I know you need a lot of time, and a good book."

"No, it's not that, Lucja," Grandpa Feliks said. "We need to talk about the carp."

"His name is Fishy, Grandpa," Lucja corrected him.

"We need to talk about Fishy."

"He's wonderful, isn't he?" Lucja said. "Maybe we can get a big bowl for him, so we don't have to wash in the sink any more."

Grandpa Feliks scratched his chin. He was amazed to find that he was nervous. After more than 40 years of Germans and Communists, an 8-year-old girl made him nervous.

"You do know why we bought the carp ... I mean – Fishy?" he asked.

Lucja turned to her grandfather.
"I know we bought him to eat," she said.
"But that was before.  He's my friend
now."

"But, Lucja, he's an *it*," Grandpa
Feliks said.  "It's a fish.  Now you run
along to your room and have a nap
before midnight mass.  Say goodbye to
Fishy."

Tears stood out in Lucja's eyes. "No, Grandpa. He's mine now. You can't eat him."

Grandpa Feliks did not take orders well. This fact had cost him three years in a Russian prison one time.

"Can't?" he said. "I will not be told *can't* in my own house. Not by Hitler. Not by Stalin. And not by you! That fish is my dinner. I will not be beaten again. I'm making a stand. Now go to your room or I will kill the fish while you watch."

Lucja's tears flowed now, as she stared up at this man she thought she knew. But she was his granddaughter, and so there was a spark of rebellion in her.

"You are just like a Communist," she said to her grandpa, then ran to her mother's apron.

# CHAPTER 9
# The Boss

Grandpa Feliks wondered if it was possible to hate a fish. He was beginning to feel it might be. All this trouble for a dinner of carp. It was stupid.

Wasn't there a time when he and his brothers had fished the rivers any time they pleased, without fear of prison? Wasn't there a time when they threw small fish back, even middle-sized fish?

He felt a need to explain to Lucja that this was about more than fish. This was about freedom to enjoy the things that grew in their own country. This was about their way of life. They were in Warsaw, not New York City.

Grandpa Feliks took a few deep breaths, then stomped down the hall to the room Lucja shared with her mother.

He went in the door, talking.

"Now listen here, Lucja," he began,
but the angry words died in his throat.
Lucja was already asleep.  Her pillow
was wet with tears.  Feliks felt his anger
drain like water from a cracked jar.

"Listen here, Lucja," he said, but softly this time.

Lucja lay sleeping with one eye half open in the strange way she had. Her cheeks were red – Grandpa Feliks could see that even in the darkness. And she got her pointed chin from her grandmother.  Grandpa Feliks's wife.

'This is very unfair,' Grandpa Feliks thought.  'What chance do I have?'

He saw Lucja for what she was. Innocent and happy.  He looked down on her with a sudden rush of love that filled his head with heat and made his hands tremble.  It was as if the world had been made for her.  Feliks reached down a single finger and touched her cheek.

'The best argument of all,' he thought. 'How is an old rebel supposed to win? She will learn sorrow soon enough. Where is the harm in letting her be happy?'

Lucja opened her other eye. "I'm not asleep, you know. I'm just pretending because I'm cross with you."

"I see," said Grandpa Feliks.  He felt like a bear with no teeth.  "Are you cross with me over Fishy?"

"Yes.  He's my best friend, and I won't eat him."

Grandpa Feliks sat on the corner of the bed.  "How could you eat him?" he said.  "He's your best friend."

Lucja knew she was winning. "I bet I look like an angel when I pretend to be asleep," she said.

"You do," her grandpa said. "Tomorrow you will look like a hungry angel."

"I don't care," Lucja cried. She sat up and hugged him. "I will think about my head instead of my tummy. Thank you, Grandpa."

"It's not for ever," Grandpa Feliks grumbled. "In a few days we will have to set him free. He will die in that bath."

"He," Grandpa Feliks said to himself. "Now I'm calling that fish *he*. Before you know it there'll be an extra place at the table for it."

"Can Fishy stay until my birthday?" Lucja asked.

Grandpa Feliks was not good with dates. "When is that?"

"April."

"April?" Grandpa Feliks spluttered. "That's four months! We can't wash in the sink for four months."

"You could dig him a pond," Lucja said. "Outside the flat."

"Are you crazy?" Grandpa Feliks asked.  "How long do you think a carp would last outside the flat?  Other people aren't as fond of Fishy as we are."

"OK," said Lucja.  "You win.  Fishy stays in the bath."

"Thank you," said Grandpa Feliks. "It's the only sensible thing to do.  But not a day past your birthday.  I mean it. I'm taking a stand."

Grandpa Feliks glanced up. Agata was at the door, smiling. Grandpa Feliks wanted to smile too – but, of course, he could not.

"Now you, go to sleep," he told Lucja. "We will wake you at 11 for church. And you, Agata, stop smiling like a simple person and make me some strong coffee. One for the fish, too, while you're about it."

"Of course, Papa," said Agata. "You're the boss."

Grandpa Feliks tucked his granddaughter in.

'The boss,' he thought. 'I wish.'

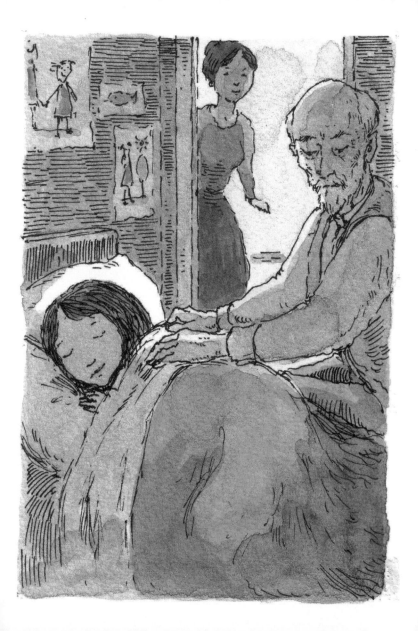

Our books are tested
for children and young people by
children and young people.

Thanks to everyone who consulted on
a manuscript for their time and effort in
helping us to make our books better
for our readers.